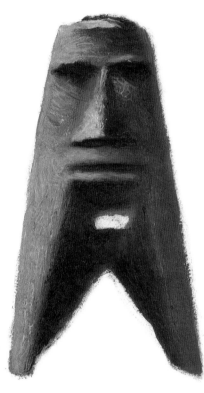

And the eagle became the sacred bird

of song, dance, and all festivity.

Sagluag, Eskimo storyteller

Adapted by Rafe Martin from a traditional Eskimo story of the same
title collected by Arctic explorer Knud Rasmussen in *The Eagle's Gift*,
Alaska Eskimo Tales. Published 1936. Now out of print.

G. P. Putnam's Sons, a division of The Putnam & Grosset Group, 200 Madison Avenue, New York, NY 10016.
G. P. Putnam's Sons, Reg. U.S. Pat. & Tm. Off. Published simultaneously in Canada. Printed in Hong Kong.
Book designed by Gunta Alexander. Text set in Veljovic.
Library-of-Congress Cataloging-in-Publication Data
Martin, Rafe, 1946–   The eagle's gift / by Rafe Martin; illustrated by Tatsuro Kiuchi.   p.   cm.
Summary: Hoping to win the return of his two brothers, an Eskimo boy follows the directions of Eagle Mother
and learns to dance, sing, and tell stories, so spreading joy throughout the world.   1. Eskimos—Alaska—Folklore.
2. Tales—Alaska. [1. Eskimos—Folklore.   2. Folklore—Alaska.] I. Kiuchi, Tatsuro, ill. II. Title.
E99.E7M315   1997   398.2'0899710798—dc20   96-3538   CIP   AC   ISBN 0-399-22923-X
1   3   5   7   9   10   8   6   4   2
First Impression

The Eagle's Gift

To the children of Seward

Best wishes!

Rafe Martin 10·97

RAFE MARTIN

ILLUSTRATED BY TATSURO KIUCHI

G. P. PUTNAM'S SONS • NEW YORK

Once, long long ago, there was a boy named Marten. His two older brothers were skilled hunters and his mother and father were proud of them. His parents had high hopes for Marten, too. Someday, like his brothers, he would be a great hunter and help his family.

One day Marten's oldest brother went off hunting and never returned. A few days after this his other brother also disappeared.

Marten's mother and father grew fearful for Marten's safety and watched over him day and night. He could not hunt alone anymore.

Marten's father liked to hunt in his kayak out on the sea, but Marten loved to roam the vast land with his bow and arrow. After a time Marten said, "Father, you must let me go my own way." At last his father agreed. Then once more Marten wandered as he pleased.

One day, as Marten roamed far from home, he saw a huge eagle circling overhead. Closer and closer swooped the eagle until it landed just before Marten. Marten was astonished. The eagle was big as a man! But he was even more astonished the next moment when the great eagle pushed back its feathered hood!

There, instead of the eagle, stood a young man wearing a shining cape of eagle feathers.

And the young man said, "Will you learn the gift of joy? Will you learn to dance and sing and tell stories that bring delight?"

"I do not understand," said Marten in a daze. "What is sing? What is dance? What is story and delight? What is joy?"

"If you agree to learn you will find out," replied the young man. "But now you must tell me yes or no. Will you or won't you? Your brothers refused and so I have not let them return. If you will learn, you can free them and bring a wondrous gift to your people. You must decide."

"Of course I will learn this thing called joy," said Marten.

"Come with me, then," replied the other.

They set off across the plain. Slowly the lands Marten knew fell behind, and the distant mountains drew closer. Marten had never been so far from home. They began climbing toward the highest peaks. Looking down, Marten could see the vast land stretching all the way back to the sea. He saw herds of caribou wandering and grazing—but they looked like tiny ants. Whales the size of minnows swam in the sea. As for men

and women, why they were almost too little to be
seen at all. The sun was bright and golden,
the sky clear and blue. Marten gazed in wonder.

As they approached the mountaintop, Marten saw a huge house perched at the edge of space. The great sky was spread overhead, and fierce winds blew all around it. A sound like the beating of a heart seemed to pulse from the rocks.

"What is that noise?" asked Marten.

"The beating of my mother's heart," replied the eagle man. "It beats loudly in expectation of sharing the gift of joy. Come, Marten," he said. He led Marten into the house. The light inside was dim. Great dark wood posts rose up high as forest trees. On a bunk in a corner perched an old eagle. She looked weak and tired. But she smiled kindly and in a faint voice like a whisper said, "It is good that you have come. The world needs joy. To bring it, you need only have a willing heart. Are you ready?"

"I am," said Marten.

"Then this is how you must start," said the old eagle mother. "For there to be joy people must learn to join together. So first you must build a feast hall where people can gather. Build it, Marten, then return." The old eagle then closed her eyes and seemed to doze.

Marten and Eagle, the eagle mother's son, went to the forest. They gathered logs, dragged them to the mountaintop, and began to build the hall. It was hard work. Very hard. At last, one day, Marten and Eagle looked at each other. They wiped the glistening sweat from their foreheads. And together they laughed, "It is done!"

When they returned, Eagle Mother looked at Marten and said, "So, joy has begun." It seemed to Marten that she sat up taller and straighter. Her pale eyes seemed a little brighter and her voice clearer. "Now that you have a hall, Marten," she continued, "you should learn to dance. Joy makes us want to get up and move, makes us want to swing our arms and legs for gladness. For this, you will need a drum. You must learn to beat upon it so that it resounds like the beating of a heart. The pulse of that drum shall set your heart free and make your blood glow. Return when this is done."

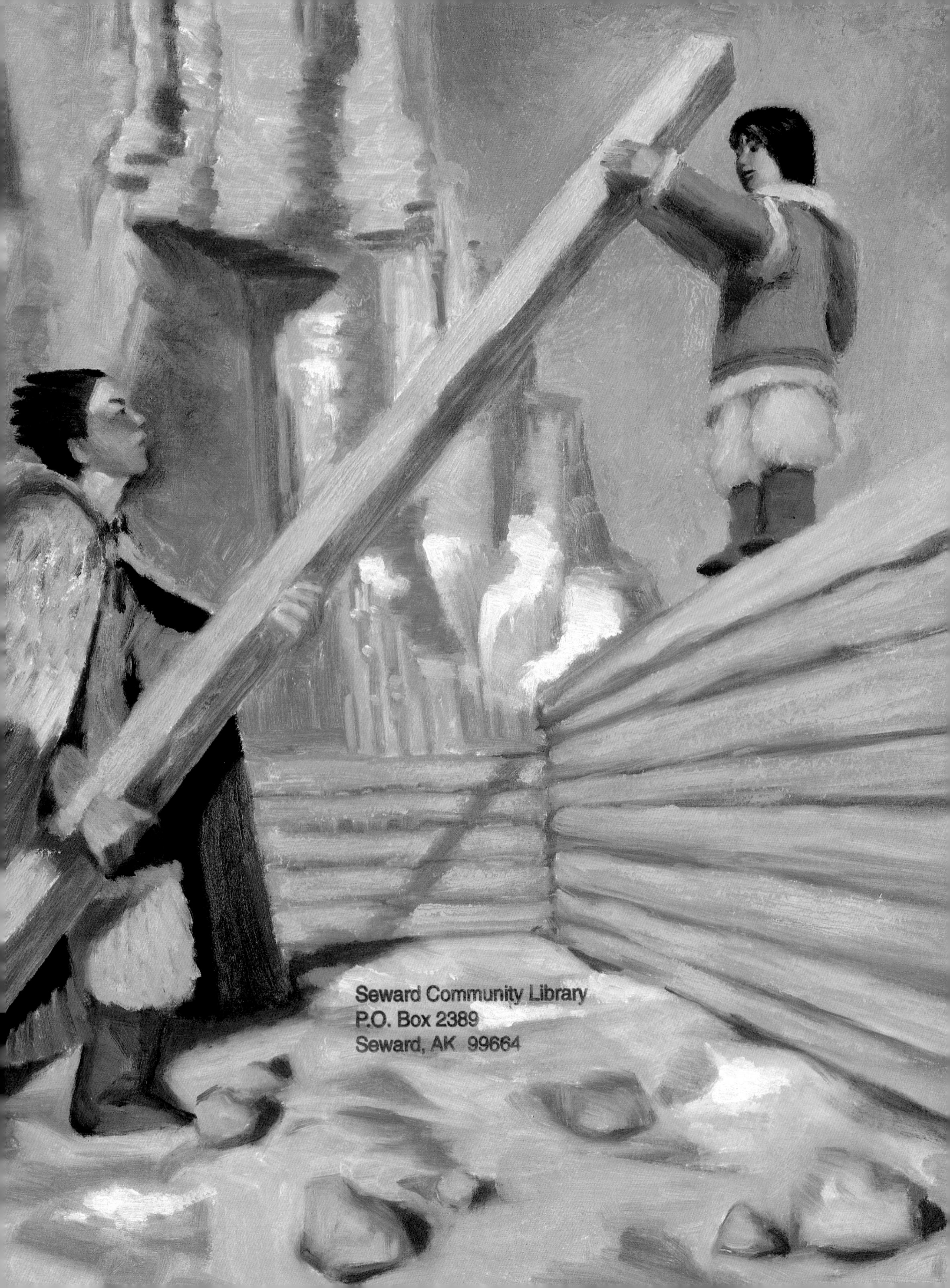

So Marten went and began to make a drum. He cut a strip of soft wood, steamed it, and little by little, carefully bent it until it was round as a hoop. He stretched a hide across its top and carved a drumstick to beat it. On the stick he painted an eagle.

He beat upon the drum, and he and Eagle leapt and shook and lifted their arms and legs. How could they not! Ah, but the wise eagle mother was so right! Marten's blood began to flow. His face glowed! As they laughed and danced, the days and nights flew by as if on eagle's wings.

"Now," said Eagle Mother when they returned, "that is *good*." Marten noticed that her once ragged feathers seemed almost smooth. "Marten," she continued, "it is time you learned to sing. Put your memories and thoughts into words that can move to the beat of your drum. This is the path of joy, Marten. Learn it, then return."

Once again Marten and Eagle went to the feast hall. Marten beat upon his drum. As he danced, he began to tell of times alone watching caribou graze and wolves at play, the wild geese flying overhead. He sang of watching his father's kayak out on the sea, whales leaping up from the water. He sang of his mother cooking, the oil lamps burning like gold. And what was this? Why, the words tumbled out high and low, not in a drone at all but full of life! His voice lifted in song! Marten knew joy! On he sang, on and on. And time flew by as if on eagle's wings.

"Yes," said Eagle Mother when they returned. "That is good. That is very, *very* good." As she spoke, she stretched out her great wings. Marten could see that all the feathers were glossy. Her eyes were bright as yellow gold and her voice rang powerfully through the hall as she said, "Marten! It is time to tell tales. You must tell of deeds and dreams, memories and wishes, fears and hopes. Tell, Marten, of times long ago and times yet to come. Let your drum beat. Let your words soar. Tell stories, Marten! Link moments together into tales and know joy."

Once again Marten did as Eagle Mother asked. Now his stories grew as he wove brief moments into long tales that came, as if by magic, to his mind then out in words through his lips. And as he told his tales, the eagle's son said, "Yes, Marten, I can see it in my mind. Ah, it brings me such joy to travel with you in words. I can see times long ago! I am among the caribou and with the wolves before the first people walked this land! I feel the warmth of the lamps of an igloo and smell good food cooking. Truly it brings joy to hear your words and, through them, to walk amidst your memories and dreams. Yes, Marten, this is a great joy!"

And together they danced and sang and told stories as time flew by. Then they returned to Eagle Mother's house.

"Marten," laughed Eagle Mother, "you have done well!" Marten looked at her and saw that she was now young and energetic, no longer old or bent or frail at all! Oh, it made him happy to see it! "Return now to the world of your people," said Eagle Mother. "Build a hall, invite friends and neighbors. Teach them to sing and dance and set fine words in order so that stories may be shared. Teach them, Marten, of these joys so that your people may live happily on this earth. Though life holds difficulties, it can also hold much joy. It is time this was known by all."

But Marten said, "We have no friends. We live alone. How shall I begin?"

"Build a feast hall," said Eagle Mother, "and friends will come. People are lonely because they do not have the gift of joy. With joy will come many friendships. Have no doubt."

Then Marten thanked Eagle Mother for her great gifts—the gifts of song and dance, of story and friendship—the things that bring joy.

"What can I offer in return?" asked Marten.

"Marten," she answered, "you have already given a great gift. I am renewed by joy. You need give nothing more."

Marten said farewell to Eagle Mother. He and Eagle walked to the mountain's edge. "Hold tight to my back, Marten," said Eagle, "and do not be afraid." Putting on his feathered hood, Eagle stretched out his wings and leapt from the cliff. Marten shut his eyes. The wind roared. Eagle beat his wings. They were falling, falling.

When Marten opened his eyes, he was standing safely back on the tundra. His friend, Eagle, stood beside him in his feathered cape, the eagle hood hanging from his shoulders. Behind them towered the great mountain on whose peak they had just stood.

"Farewell," said Marten. "I shall never forget all you have taught me nor the many songs and dances, the joy we discovered together. You are my first friend."

"When the hall is built and joy is given, then you shall see your brothers once more," said Eagle. "Farewell, my friend. I, too, shall never forget you." Then Marten watched as his friend flew up, circling higher and higher until he was just a speck in the sky. And then he was gone.

Marten set off again on the long journey home.

When Marten returned, his parents wept and cried over him. They had feared that, like his brothers, he would never return. Then Marten told them his tale and said, "We must build a hall and share the gifts of joy. Then my brothers will return."

"Are you sure, Marten?" they asked. "And what is joy?"

"Let all of us work together," answered Marten, "and you shall see."

So Marten and his father and mother dragged great logs from the forest. Building the hall took time and was very hard work. At last the task was done. They looked at one another, and they smiled.

Then Marten made a drum and began to beat upon it. He hopped this way and that, moving his legs and arms. His mother and father looked at each other in amazement. They began to laugh. They danced with Marten in joy. He taught them to sing. They sang in joy! He showed them how to put fine words together to build stories that amaze the mind with beauty, laughter, and tears. Oh, what joy they had laughing, singing, dancing, and sharing stories.

"Now Mother, Father," said Marten, "we must invite guests."

Soon many people began to appear wearing the skins of bobcat, wolf, lynx, bear, and fox. And in the crowd heading toward the hall came Marten's two brothers! It was just as Eagle Mother had said. The people streamed into the hall. Marten beat upon the drum. He sang and told stories. The people ate and laughed. After a time, the guests also got up. They too danced and sang and told stories. Many nights and days flew by as if on eagle's wings.

At last the time came for the guests to depart and return again to their own homes. Wonderful gifts were exchanged. "But nothing," the people all agreed, "nothing, no gift we can give, can compare with this great gift of joy!"

As the guests left the hall, they dropped down onto their four legs and raced away across the snow. Bobcat, wolf, lynx, bear, caribou, and white arctic fox—the animals themselves had come as the first guests to the first feast hall! Lighthearted and fleet, they now raced away to carry forth the wonderful message of joy.

And so joy spread through all the world.

Festivity cannot be enjoyed with song and dance alone.
The most festive thing is joy in beautiful words and our ability to express them.

Apakag, Eskimo storyteller

The source for this story can be found in an out-of-print collection titled *The Eagle's Gift*. The stories in it were gathered more than seventy years ago by Knud Rasmussen, a Dane with Eskimo ancestry and one of the great Arctic explorers. He was, by all accounts, a daring, sympathetic, imaginative man and a lover of good stories. Sagluag, an Eskimo storyteller from the Colville River area of Alaska, told him a version of the tale. It presents the mythic origins of the midwinter Messenger or Barter Feast, an annual event celebrated with gift-giving, song, dance, feasting, and storytelling.

The story reveals that friendship and community are real foundations of joy. So while life may be difficult, there is also much that is truly joyful. This wisdom has come to us from our wise and compassionate teachers—the animals. And it reminds us that, even as we humans need joy, the natural world needs human effort if it is to be renewed. All life is connected.

Since early times the peoples of the Arctic have lived with good humor and tremendous skill in one of the harshest physical environments on this earth and have found joy there. Because they speak from such experience, we, in our materially affluent but often joyless societies, might do well to listen.

This book, then, is for them and for the inspiration their lives and stories offer. It is for the birds and animals, too. Even when I was a child their presence filled me with joy.

Note: Eskimo is an Algonquin term meaning "raw-flesh eaters." Innuit is the name more generally used among these people for themselves and means simply "the people."